Puffin Books

THE MERMAID AT No. 13

Hamlet Orlando Julius Caesar Brown has a problem, and it isn't his name. It's the mermaid in the bath.

There she sits, as large as life, combing her long hair and swishing her tail to and fro! Hamlet can't think what to do, so he decides, very sensibly, to ask a policeman. But neither the policeman nor his family believe him.

At last Hamlet gets the evidence he needs and he's wondering what to do with it when he has an absolutely, brilliantly, wonderfully, gloriously good idea!

Gyles Brandreth is the author of many books of quizzes, puzzles, games and jokes. He is also a well-known children's television personality. He lives in London with his wife and three children.

Other books by Gyles Brandreth

GYLES BRANDRETH

THE MERMAID AT
No. 13

ILLUSTRATED BY JULIE TENNENT

PUFFIN BOOKS

PUFFIN BOOKS

Published by the Penguin Group
Penguin Books Ltd, 27 Wrights Lane, London W8 5TZ, England
Penguin Books USA Inc., 375 Hudson Street, New York, New York 10014, USA
Penguin Books Australia Ltd, Ringwood, Victoria, Australia
Penguin Books Canada Ltd, 10 Alcorn Avenue, Toronto, Ontario, Canada M4V 3B2
Penguin Books (NZ) Ltd, 182–190 Wairau Road, Auckland 10, New Zealand

Penguin Books Ltd, Registered Offices: Harmondsworth, Middlesex, England

First published by Viking Kestrel 1989
Published in Puffin Books 1990
10 9 8 7 6 5 4

Printed in England by Clays Ltd, St Ives plc
Filmset in Palatino (Linotron 202)

1. The Mermaid in the Bath

Hamlet Orlando Julius Caesar Brown had a problem. And it wasn't his name. It was the mermaid in the bath.

Hamlet was nine years old and lived at No. 13 Irving Terrace, Hammersmith, West London, with his mother and his father and his goodie-goodie eleven-year-old sister Susan. And now it seemed with a mermaid as well. He could hardly believe his eyes, but there was no doubt about it. There she was, this mermaid, sitting in the bath, swishing her long tail to and fro and combing her very long golden hair with what looked exactly like Mrs Brown's best comb.

It was just after breakfast on an ordinary

Monday morning at the beginning of the last week of the summer holidays. Hamlet had only gone into the bathroom to clean his teeth. He didn't always remember to brush his teeth after breakfast. Today he was rather sorry he had remembered, because now here he was standing in the bathroom face to face with a real live mermaid and he hadn't a clue what to do.

Well, what *do* you do when you find a mermaid in the bath? If you're Hamlet

Brown, you take a good look, swallow hard, turn round and run out of the room as fast as you can, closing the door behind you.

Hamlet stood on the landing wondering what to do next. Perhaps he should go back in and ask the mermaid what she thought she was doing sitting in the Brown's bath at 9.15 on a Monday morning in September. He took a deep breath and began to turn the handle when he remembered that his parents were always telling him not to talk to strangers and this mermaid was certainly the strangest stranger he'd ever seen.

Hamlet put his eye to the keyhole. On the other side of the door the key was in the lock so he couldn't see anything. But he could hear something. Was the mermaid talking? It didn't sound like English, but perhaps mermaids don't speak English. Was she singing? Hamlet had a vague idea that mermaids are supposed to spend a lot of time singing. And people do sing in the bath. Mr Brown always sang in the bath, but then Mr Brown was an actor and he would sing whenever and wherever he could. (Last Christmas Mr Brown sang the whole of 'Good King Wenceslas' at the top of his voice on the top deck of the number nine bus and Hamlet and Susan nearly died of embarrassment.)

Hamlet listened at the bathroom door more carefully. The mermaid wasn't singing. She was giggling.

'I don't like the sound of that,' said Hamlet to himself and he scampered downstairs to find his parents. He ran into the kitchen to look for his mother but she wasn't there. Then he remembered that she was out at work this morning.

Mrs Brown was an actress too, but she didn't appear on the stage in plays like Mr Brown. She specialized in recording the voices that go with radio and TV

commercials and this morning she'd set off
early to go to the recording studio. She was
only going to record seven words today –
'Whizzo washes whitest and brightest and
best!' – but those seven words would earn

her a lot of money because she would be paid every time the advertisement using her voice was shown on TV.

Mr Brown wasn't earning any money this week because he didn't have a job at the moment. When actors aren't working they say they're 'resting'. Mr Brown had just finished appearing in a play about Noah and his Ark at the Open Air Theatre in Regent's Park and soon he was going to be the Mad Hatter in a musical version of *Alice in Wonderland*, but at present he was 'resting'. Mrs Brown had said to him very sternly at breakfast, 'Now you're resting you can get some odd jobs done around the house. It's years since we cleared out the attic, you know.'

'Clearing out the attic doesn't sound very restful,' said Mr Brown, 'but I'll do my best, oh light of my life.' Mr Brown always talked as if he was in the theatre in the middle of a very dramatic play even if he was only in the kitchen in the middle of his second piece of toast and marmalade.

Mr Brown wasn't in the kitchen now. And he wasn't in the sitting-room either. And he wasn't in the broom cupboard underneath the stairs because Hamlet looked in there as well. (As it happens, Mr Brown was in the garden, but Hamlet didn't think to look for him there.)

'Where is he?' wondered Hamlet, who was beginning to feel a little nervous. He ran back up the stairs, skidded past the bathroom door and went into his parents' bedroom. No sign of Mr Brown there.

'Where could he have got to?' thought Hamlet. Then he had a brainwave. 'The attic! He's in the attic, clearing it out like Mum said he should.'

Feeling a lot happier Hamlet ran out of his parents' room and up the stairs to the top floor. There, sure enough, on the landing he found a step-ladder under the trap door in the ceiling that led to the attic. The trap door was open.

Hamlet had never been into the attic before and he wasn't sure he wanted to go into it now, but he needed to find his father and he needed to find him fast so he climbed the step-ladder and poked his head through the trap door. The attic was very dark, but he could see enough to be certain that Mr Brown wasn't there.

Mum was right, the place was very dusty and very, very untidy. There were boxes full of old books, and suitcases full of old clothes, and odd bits of furniture here, there and everywhere. And cobwebs too. And a strange, sinister, gurgling noise. It was only the water tank, but Hamlet didn't like the sound of it. It was almost as alarming as the giggling mermaid.

Poor Hamlet really was quite frightened by now. Slowly he clambered down the step-ladder. What was he going to do? His bedroom and Susan's bedroom were both on the top floor. He looked into his own room, but Mr Brown wasn't there. He went to Susan's room. Stuck on to the door was a giant sign that read: THIS IS SUSAN BROWN'S BEDROOM. KINDLY DO NOT DISTURB.

Hamlet never felt very kindly towards Susan. There was nothing wrong with her really. That was the problem. Everybody

(especially her teachers) thought that Susan Brown was a perfect child. Everybody, that is, except for Hamlet who thought that Susan Brown was a perfect pest.

Hamlet knew that Susan had put up the DO NOT DISTURB sign just to keep him out of her room and when he'd first seen the sign he'd thought to himself, 'I don't want to go into her stupid room anyway.' But now he did want to go in there. He *did* want to see his sister. He knocked on the

door, 'Susan! Susan! Are you in there?'
There was no answer. He turned the handle
on the door and pushed. The door was
locked.

'Help!' thought Hamlet, 'I'm alone in a
house with a mad mermaid! Help! What am
I going to do?'

Then Hamlet had an idea.

2. The Policeman at the Door

As fast as his legs could carry him, Hamlet
ran down the stairs. He skidded past the
bathroom door with his eyes shut tight and
almost fell down the next flight of stairs he
was in such a hurry. He raced into the
kitchen and grabbed the telephone.

With his heart thumping, he lifted the
receiver and then, very carefully, he dialled
999.

'This is the emergency operator,' said a
voice on the telephone. 'Which service do
you require – police, fire or ambulance?'

'Police,' said Hamlet without hesitating.

'I'm putting you through,' said the
operator. There was a moment's pause, a
click and another voice came on the line.

'Police emergencies. Can I help you?'

'Yes,' said Hamlet. 'There's a mermaid in my bath and I don't know what to do about it!'

'I'm sorry, I didn't quite catch that. What did you say?'

'I said there's a mermaid in my bath,' said Hamlet as loudly and as clearly as he could.

'Oh dear,' said the voice. 'Where are you?'

'No. 13 Irving Terrace, Hammersmith.'

'And what's your name?' asked the voice.

'Hamlet,' said Hamlet.

'Right, Mr Hamlet. We'll send someone round straight away.'

Hamlet decided he didn't want to stay in the house any longer. He thought he'd go and wait on the doorstep. He went to the front door, opened it and who should he find there but Mr Brown, all dressed up in his gardening clothes. (Mr Brown loved dressing up, so when he was gardening he didn't just wear bright yellow gardening boots and bright orange gardening gloves and a bright green gardening apron, he wore a bright red, white and blue woolly hat with a pink pompom on as well.)

'What's up with you, my boy?' said Mr Brown looking at Hamlet's anxious face.

'You seem very pale. Have you seen a ghost or something?'

'No,' said Hamlet who thought he was about to burst into tears, 'I've seen a mermaid!'

'A what?' said Mr Brown, who thought his hearing must be going and pulled off his woolly hat.

'A mermaid,' said Hamlet. He was about to explain everything to his bewildered Dad when they heard the wailing sound of a police siren – bee-baa, bee-baa, bee-baa – closely followed by the squeal of brakes as a police car swept round the bend and into Irving Terrace. It screeched to a halt outside No. 13 and a policeman leapt out.

He ran straight up the little garden path and grabbed hold of Mr Brown who yelped 'Unhold me, man!'

'Is this him?' the policeman asked Hamlet.

'No,' said Hamlet, 'that's my Dad.'

'Oh,' said the policeman, letting go of Mr Brown but giving his funny gardening clothes a very suspicious look, 'I thought he might have been the madman.'

'What madman?' asked Mr Brown, who

was beginning to feel that he might be going crazy as well as deaf.

'The madman in the bath,' said the policeman.

'It isn't a madman,' said Hamlet. 'It's – or rather she's – a mermaid.'

'A mermaid?' said the policeman. 'Are you sure, young man?'

'Yes,' said Hamlet, very solemnly.

'You mean a real mermaid, with a tail and long hair and what have you?' asked the policeman.

'Yes,' said Hamlet, and he said it with such a serious air that the policeman believed him.

'Well, well, well,' he said, shaking his head. 'I thought I'd seen it all, but a mermaid's something I've not come across before. This is going to be interesting.'

'It certainly is,' said Mr Brown.

'Lead the way young man,' said the policeman.

And Hamlet and Mr Brown and the policeman (who was called Constable Copper by the way – he was, *he really was*) went into the house and up the stairs and stopped outside the bathroom door.

'In here you say, young man?'

'Yes,' said Hamlet.

'Very good,' said Constable Copper. 'Stand to one side please, gentlemen. I'll go in first.' He put his hand on the door handle and was beginning to turn it when he had a thought.

'Did you say it was a lady mermaid?'

Hamlet nodded.

'Then I'd better knock,' said the policeman. He tapped gently on the bathroom door. 'Excuse me, madam, can you hear me?' There was no reply. 'Excuse me, madam,' said the policeman, rather more loudly this time. 'This is P.C. Copper of the Metropolitan Police here. I have reason to believe that you are trespassing in somebody else's bath. Do you have anything to say?'

Silence.

'I'm going in,' said the policeman. He turned the handle and with a firm shove pushed open the door. The bath was empty. The bathroom was empty.

'Let's face it,' said the policeman looking at Hamlet with an eyebrow raised, 'there's nobody here.'

'But there was,' said Hamlet, 'I promise you there was.'

'That's as may be,' said Constable Copper, 'but there isn't now. Perhaps your mermaid slipped through the plughole, perhaps she made her escape down the loo, or perhaps you've been watching too many of these fantasy films on the telly.'

Hamlet didn't know what to say. Mr Brown didn't know what to say either, but he felt he had to say something, so he said, 'You know, Constable, I was Sherlock

Holmes once upon a time.'

'Oh really, sir,' said the policeman raising his other eyebrow and moving quickly out of the bathroom and down the stairs. 'This house is full of lunatics,' he thought to himself as he made his way back to his car.

'No, you misunderstand me,' said Mr Brown. 'I don't mean I used to *be* Sherlock Holmes, I mean that once I played the part of Sherlock Holmes in a play about the great detective. You see, I'm an actor.'

'Ah well,' said the policeman clambering into his car, 'that explains everything.'

'Oh good,' said Mr Brown who didn't think it explained anything.

The policeman started up the engine. 'Can I give you a word of advice, sir?' he said to Mr Brown. 'I think that boy of yours needs to watch a little less television. Give

him a few more early nights and I think
he'll see a few fewer mermaids. Goodbye.'

And P.C. Copper drove off leaving
Mr Brown and Hamlet standing on the
pavement feeling fairly foolish.

'But there was a mermaid in the bath,
Dad, there was, there was, *there was*!'

3. A Marrow in the Garden

When Mrs Brown returned home at lunchtime and heard all about the goings-on at No. 13 that morning she was not amused.

'Hamlet, what on earth made you pretend to see a mermaid in the bath?' she asked her son who was sitting very sulkily at the end of the kitchen table.

'I didn't pretend,' said Hamlet; 'I did see a mermaid and that's that.'

Mrs Brown shook her head and sighed and passed a bowl of tomato soup to her husband who took it from her, blew her a kiss and said, 'Thank you, oh sweet one, for this fair repast.'

Mr Brown liked to talk in this funny,

theatrical way. Mrs Brown found it silly and
irritating. Rather crossly she said to her
husband, 'And what were you doing while
your son was busy mermaid-spotting?
Snoozing, I bet!'

'Far from it, my sweet,' said Mr Brown
who was used to Mrs Brown being cross

with him. 'I am happy to tell you I was doing something very useful.'

'Like clearing out the attic?'

'Well, no,' said Mr Brown looking a little shamefaced. 'As it happens I was in the garden.'

'Good. Doing some weeding?'

'Well, no,' said Mr Brown looking even more shamefaced. 'As it happens, I was looking after my marrow.'

'Oh really,' said Mrs Brown looking crosser than ever now. 'You and that marrow!'

Mr Brown was very proud of his marrow. It was the only vegetable he had ever tried to grow in the garden. Mrs Brown didn't believe in growing vegetables in a tiny London garden because, she said, the soil was full of lead from the traffic fumes. She was also cross about the marrow because Mr Brown had chosen to grow it right in the middle of a bed full of nasturtiums which

happened to be Mrs Brown's favourite flowers.

'When I win the prize for growing the

biggest and most beautiful marrow in Hammersmith I think you'll change your tune,' said Mr Brown in a dignified voice.

Mrs Brown tut-tutted and sighed one of her biggest sighs. She took her own bowl of soup and sat down next to Susan. 'Well, Susan, while the men folk have been making merry with their mermaids and their marrows, what have you been up to?'

'I've been working on my holiday project, Mum,' said Susan sweetly.

'That's more like it,' said Mrs Brown. 'At least there's one sensible member of the Brown family.'

'How's it going?' asked Mr Brown.

'I've nearly finished,' said Susan, with a pretty smile. Hamlet thought he was going to be sick. He was supposed to do a holiday project as well, but of course he hadn't even started his.

'What's the project about this time, Susan?' asked Mr Brown, who really should have known because Susan had told him lots and lots of times.

'It's about fishes, Dad.'

'Just fishes?' sneered Hamlet.

'Oh no, all kinds of sea creatures. I did a page about dolphins today. Did you know that dolphins always keep one eye open when they are asleep?'

'Boring!' said Hamlet very rudely.

'I don't suppose you've got a page about mermaids, have you Susan?' asked Mrs Brown with a wink.

Susan giggled.

'Oh do shut up, Susan,' said Hamlet. 'I don't care if you don't believe me. I saw a mermaid in the bath this morning and that's that.'

'And last summer you saw a ghost in your bedroom,' said Susan.

'Yes, I did, if you must know. And you saw it too, Susan. Don't pretend you didn't.'

'I might have seen a ghost and then again I might not!' said Susan who honestly wasn't sure if she really had seen a ghost last summer or only dreamt it.

'Stop bickering, you two,' said Mrs Brown. 'If you've finished your soup you can take the bowls to the sink. It's your turn to wash up, Hamlet. Susan and I have got work to do.'

'Oh really,' said Mr Brown, 'anything interesting?'

'Yes,' said Mrs Brown. 'We've got to rehearse!'

'Rehearse, eh? This sounds exciting. Tell us more.'

'Well,' said Mrs Brown, 'you know this morning I went to do one of my voice-overs' – recording the words that went with a television commercial was what Mrs Brown called 'doing one of her voice-overs' – 'well, I've got to do another one this afternoon.'

'Good show!' said Mr Brown who was delighted at the thought of the extra money Mrs Brown would be earning.

'But why does Susan have to rehearse as well?' asked Hamlet from the sink.

'Because they want an eleven-year-old girl to do the recording as well.'

'Oh no,' said Hamlet, 'it's just not fair.'

'Oh yes,' said Susan, who had wanted to be an actress ever since she was seven.

'You haven't got to say a lot,' explained Mrs Brown, 'but you'll get paid for it.'

'How much?' asked Hamlet.

'Thirty pounds!' said Mrs Brown.

'Oh my!' said Susan, grinning from ear to ear.

'What a swizz!' said Hamlet, scowling from top to toe.

'I've brought the script home for us to look at,' said Mrs Brown rummaging in her handbag. 'Here we are. This is what I have to say: "Try the tingle tongue taste test and you'll find that tip-top Trolloppe's best baked beans always beat the rest."'

'That sounds really stupid,' said Hamlet who decided there and then that the one thing he would never, ever, ever, EVER eat again in the whole of his life – even if he was starving and it was the very last thing left to eat on the face of the planet earth – was Trolloppe's best baked beans.

'What do I have to say, Mum?' asked Susan.

Mrs Brown showed her the script; 'Yes, Trolloppe's the best.'

'I don't believe it,' said Hamlet, who was furious now. 'I don't believe it. Do you mean to say she's going to get thirty pounds for saying just four words? I want to be sick.'

'Come now, Hamlet, that's not a very nice way to speak,' said Mr Brown. 'Let's leave Mum and Susan to rehearse. You can help me in the garden. If you're very good I might let you use my instant camera to take a photograph of my prize marrow.'

Hamlet's face brightened a little. He'd been wanting to have a go with the instant camera ever since Mr Brown got it at Christmas.

'And if you take a very good photograph I might even pay you for it,' said Mr Brown with a chuckle.

'Thirty pounds?' asked Hamlet, hopefully.

'Thirty pence more likely,' said his father. 'Come on.'

With a shrug of his shoulders and a sideways sneer at his sister, Hamlet followed Mr Brown out of the kitchen and into the garden.

4. 'Trolloppe's Best Baked·Beans'

At half past two that afternoon Mrs Brown and Susan set off for the studio to record their voice-over.

The studio was in the heart of the West End of London, in Soho, just off Piccadilly Circus. Mr Brown had suggested that they go by car, but Mrs Brown didn't like taking the car into the middle of town. 'It takes ages to find anywhere to park,' she said, 'and then if you're not very careful you end up with a parking ticket and a fine. We'll go on the underground. It'll be easier and quicker.'

It was. From Hammersmith to Piccadilly Circus was just eight stops and it took Mrs Brown and Susan exactly thirty minutes to make the journey from door to door.

Susan had expected the studio to be large and swish and in a big modern building. In fact, it was small and up some fairly rickety steps in a tall, narrow, dark building just behind a theatre where Mrs Brown said Mr Brown had once appeared as the back legs of a cow in pantomime.

The outside of the building was dingy

and old, but the studio itself, though small
and dark, was very modern.

Susan and Mrs Brown were greeted by
the producer, a tall, thin man who wore
green trousers, a stripy green shirt and a
ginger beard. He called Mrs Brown
'Darling!' which Susan didn't like. And he
called Susan 'Sweetie!' which she liked
even less. Everyone called him Rod and he
was obviously in charge.

'Have you done a voice-over before,
sweetie?' he asked Susan.

'No,' said Susan, 'but I want to be an
actress.'

'If you're anything like your darling
mamma,' said Rod, sounding just like Mr
Brown, 'you'll be the best in the business.'
Susan liked that. Rod then kissed Mrs
Brown on the cheek, which Susan did not
like.

'This way ladies, please,' said Rod and he
led Mrs Brown and Susan through a heavy

door into a small room where two other people were sitting at a long desk covered with knobs and levers and dials.

'This,' said Rod, 'is the control room, where I shall be master-minding your performance, sweetie, and through here' – and he led Susan and Mrs Brown through another even heavier door into an even smaller room – 'is where you're going to be giving us your all.'

'Is this the studio?' asked Susan looking around the little room and feeling a bit disappointed. She had expected bright lights and a team of technicians and

perhaps even a camera or two. Instead there was a table, two chairs, one microphone, one glass of water, and two pairs of headphones.

'Make yourselves comfortable, girls,' said Rod. 'If you pop on the headphones you'll be able to hear what I'm saying when I'm back in there.'

Rod returned to the control room and Susan and her mother sat down and put on the headphones.

'OK, darling,' said Rod's voice, 'when you're ready we'll start with you. Take your time.'

Mrs Brown laid the script on the table, cleared her throat and began to read: 'Try the tingle tongue taste test and you'll find that tip-top Trolloppe's best baked beans always beat the test.'

'No, darling,' wailed Rod through the headphones, 'it's not beat the *test*, it's beat the *rest*!'

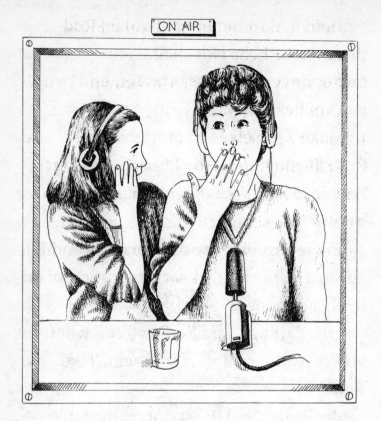

'Sorry, Rod,' said Mrs Brown.

'Not to worry, darling. Go again, when you're ready.'

Mrs Brown swallowed hard and had another go. 'Try the tingle tongue taste test and you'll find that tip-top Trolloppe's blest blaked bleans . . .'

'Hold it, darling, hold it!' called Rod through the headphones.

'I'm sorry, Rod,' said Mrs Brown.

'Don't worry, darling, it's a terrible tongue-twister.'

'I like tongue-twisters,' said Susan, who had once won a fifty pence off Mr Brown for saying 'The sixth sick Sheikh's sixth sheep's sick' sixty-six times without making a single slip.

'OK, sweetie,' said Rod, 'why don't you give it a go?'

'Can I Mum?' said Susan.

'Of course, that's what you're here for,' said Mrs Brown with a laugh.

'Ready when you are, sweetie,' said Rod.

Susan took a deep breath and said: 'Try the tingle tongue taste test and you'll find that tip-top Trolloppe's best baked beans always beat the rest.'

'Bingo!' said Rod, 'you've got it in one. Brill!'

'Well done, Susan,' said Mrs Brown.

'We'll give your mum your line now, sweetie. OK?' said Rod.

'Of course,' said Susan who was feeling very pleased with herself. (Well, it was a bit of a mouthful, and she had managed it perfectly first time around. Could you have done it without making a mistake? Could you? Have a go . . . 'Try the tingle tongue taste test and you'll find that tip-top

Trolloppe's best baked beans always beat the rest.')

'OK, darling, in your own time,' said Rod.

'Yes, Trolloppe's the best,' said Mrs Brown.

'And so are you,' said Rod. 'That's a wrap, everybody. Thank you very much.'

'Is that it?' asked Susan who was just beginning to enjoy herself.

'Yes, that's it,' said Mrs Brown.

'It never takes long when you're working with true professionals, sweetie,' said Rod as he ushered them out of the studio. 'Bye-bye darling, wonderful as always,' he said to Mrs Brown and he kissed her on the cheek. 'Bye-bye sweetie, you were just perfect. We'll be hearing more from you I know. Bye!'

Susan and Mrs Brown made their way out of the dark studio building into the sunny street where the sun was so bright that it made them blink. They would probably have blinked anyway because who should they see, coming towards the building just as they were coming out of it, but Mr Brown and Hamlet.

'Surprise, surprise!' said Mr Brown. 'Was it a triumph, girls?'

'It certainly was,' said Mrs Brown. 'I kept fluffing my lines, so Susan took over and saved the day.'

'It was great fun,' said Susan.

'But what are you two doing here?' asked Mrs Brown who had hoped that Mr Brown and Hamlet would have been busy doing something useful, like cleaning out the attic, rather than gallivanting around the West End of London.

'We've come to give you a lift home, that's what we're doing,' said Mr Brown. 'After your afternoon labours we thought you'd appreciate being driven home by chauffeur, so here we are.'

'Thank you very much,' said Mrs Brown.

'Thanks Dad,' said Susan. 'Where's the car?'

'Just round the corner. Follow me,' said Mr Brown. 'We were very lucky. We found a perfect place to park only fifty yards down the road.'

'But it's double yellow lines all round here,' said Mrs Brown.

'Have no fear, my dear. Trust your husband. Have I ever let you down?'

Mrs Brown didn't reply, but followed Hamlet and Mr Brown to the end of the street where they turned left and, sure enough, there on the corner was the Brown family car. And there standing by it was a traffic warden, notebook in hand, pencil poised, busily writing out a parking ticket.

'Oh no,' said Mr Brown.

'Oh Dad,' said Hamlet.

'Oh dear,' said Susan.

Mrs Brown said nothing – which was nice of her. She could have said, 'I told you so.'

5. 'At Last – The Evidence!'

The next day was Tuesday and, after breakfast, everybody at No. 13 Irving Terrace had something to do except for Hamlet. Hamlet was feeling grumpy. Hamlet was feeling bored.

'I'm going out to do some shopping,' said Mrs Brown, 'why don't you come with me?'

'No thanks,' said Hamlet.

'I'm going to do a little work in the garden,' said Mr Brown. 'Come and help.'

'Can I take some more photos?' asked Hamlet.

'We've got eleven pictures of the marrow already,' said Mr Brown. 'It's a beautiful specimen, but I think eleven pictures are enough.'

'You could always read a book,' said Mrs Brown putting on her coat.

'I don't feel like reading a book,' said Hamlet.

'Why don't you read the newspaper instead?' suggested Mr Brown, trying to be helpful and passing the local paper over to his son. It was the *Hammersmith Times*, which is an excellent paper, but it has to be admitted that it doesn't always have a lot in it to interest nine-year-old boys.

'I don't feel like reading the paper,' said Hamlet.

'You can lend me a hand with my project if you like. I've got to draw a lot of pictures this morning – starfish and turtles and crabs and things.'

'No thanks,' said Hamlet who certainly wasn't interested in helping his goodie-goodie sister with her rotten project.

'You'd find it very interesting,' said Susan. 'I bet you didn't know that a starfish has an eye on the end of each of its arms.'

'Everybody knows that!' said Hamlet, sticking his tongue out at his sister.

'Well, don't help me then,' said Susan. 'I can manage quite well on my own, thank you very much.'

'Humph,' said Hamlet.

Susan didn't say anything, but gave her parents each a kiss and then ran off up to her room to get on with the project. Last summer her project had been on the subject of the human body and, of course, her teacher said it was the best project in the

class. Hamlet knew that this new project of Susan's would come top as well. Sometimes he really hated his sister. She was such a clever-clogs.

Mrs Brown set off on her shopping expedition and Mr Brown dressed up in his funny gardening clothes – yellow boots, orange gloves, green apron, red, white and blue pompom hat and all – and went out into the garden to look at his marrow. It really was a very, very big one. 'Very beautiful too,' thought Mr Brown.

Hamlet couldn't think what to do. As Mrs Brown had closed the front door behind her she'd called out, 'Don't forget to brush your teeth,' so Hamlet thought he might as well do that.

He climbed the stairs to the bathroom and was just turning the handle of the bathroom door when he thought he heard a noise coming from inside. He bent down and put his ear to the keyhole and listened. Yes, no doubt about it, the mermaid was back!

What was he going to do this time? He certainly wasn't going to tell Susan. And he didn't think he could really ring the police. He'd have to go and get his dad.

Hamlet pressed his ear as close to the keyhole as he could to make absolutely sure. There was no doubt at all. She was in there and this time he was going to catch her.

Quickly and quietly he tiptoed down the stairs. He was just about to open the front door to go into the garden when on the little table in the hallway, sitting on top of a pile of gloves, old letters and last week's newspapers, he saw Mr Brown's instant camera. In a flash, Hamlet had an idea.

He picked up the camera and checked to see if there was any film left. Yes, just one picture to go. This was exactly what Hamlet needed. The clever thing about the instant camera was that the moment you'd taken the photograph out popped the picture.

Still on tiptoe and as quickly and quietly as he had come down the stairs Hamlet climbed up again. He put his ear to the door once more. Good, she was still there.

Carefully he hung the camera around his neck. He took a deep breath and put both hands on the handle of the door. One, two, three, and in he went.

And there she was, the very same mermaid, sitting in the very same bath, swishing the very same tail from side to side, and combing that very long golden hair of hers with Mrs Brown's best comb.

Yesterday Hamlet couldn't believe his eyes. Today he couldn't believe his luck. Now he wasted no time. He lifted the camera, looked through the viewfinder, and pressed the button. Click, flash, whirr, the photo was taken!

The mermaid let out a little squeal of distress. Hamlet let out a little cry of triumph, turned on his heels and ran out of the room, slamming the door tight shut behind him. With the camera swinging round his neck and the picture held tightly in his hand, he raced down the stairs and into the kitchen.

'At last, I've got the evidence!' he shouted, but nobody heard him of course because Mrs Brown was out shopping, Mr Brown was in the garden and Susan was up in her bedroom getting on with her project.

Hamlet sat down at the kitchen table. Now he wasn't bored at all. He was very, very excited. But he wasn't sure what he should do. Should he wait for Mrs Brown to come home? Should he try telephoning Constable Copper? Should he go and find

his father in the garden? He was wondering
what best to do next when he had an idea,
an absolutely, brilliantly, wonderfully,
gloriously good idea...

6. 'Hold the Front Page!'

On Wednesday morning that week, at the offices of the *Hammersmith Times*, the editor of the weekly newspaper, Mr Samuel Sign, was feeling very glum. Mr Sign was unhappy because he didn't have a really good story for this week's front page. It was the end of the summer holidays and not much of note seemed to be happening in Hammersmith.

Last week, when a cat had climbed on to the roof of the town hall and been rescued by the fire brigade, the paper had an exciting front page picture of a fireman with the cat tucked into his jacket as he climbed down the ladder. And the week before, when a local lady had celebrated her

hundredth birthday, the paper had a
wonderful picture of her blowing out every
one of her hundred candles with a single
puff. But this week, nothing!

Samuel Sign – known in the trade as Sign
of the *Times* – was scratching his head,
wondering what on earth he was going to
do, when his secretary came in with the
post.

'I think you'll like the first letter,' she said. And he did.

The letter was from Master Hamlet Brown of 13 Irving Terrace, Hammersmith, and this is what it said:

DEAR MR EDITOR (OR IS IT MRS EDITOR? BECAUSE I DON'T KNOW YOUR NAME I CAN'T BE SURE. IF I'VE GOT IT WRONG, SORRY. GO ON READING PLEASE ANYWAY!)

Mr Sign went on reading.

I AM WRITING TO YOU BECAUSE I HAVE A WORLD EXCLUSIVE STORY FOR YOU AND I THINK YOU WILL FIND IT VERY EXCITING.

'A world exclusive,' chortled Samuel Sign, 'how wonderful!'

ON MONDAY MORNING, AFTER BREAKFAST, I WENT INTO THE BATHROOM AT HOME TO BRUSH MY TEETH.

'Yes, yes,' muttered Mr Sign.

I LIVE WITH MY PARENTS BY THE
WAY. THEY ARE ACTORS. THAT'S WHY
I'M CALLED HAMLET. MY DAD WAS
IN A PLAY CALLED HAMLET WHEN I
WAS BORN.

'Lucky he wasn't in Worzel Gummidge,'
thought Mr Sign.
I'VE ALSO GOT A SISTER CALLED
SUSAN BUT I DON'T THINK YOU'D BE
VERY INTERESTED IN HER. SHE
THINKS SHE'S VERY INTERESTING, OF
COURSE, BUT SHE ISN'T. YOU CAN
TAKE THAT FROM ME.

'Oh dear,' sighed Mr Sign, 'I wish he'd
come to the point.'
THE POINT IS –

'Ah good!'
I WENT INTO THE BATHROOM AFTER
BREAKFAST TO BRUSH MY TEETH
AND WHAT DID I FIND SITTING IN
THE BATH?

'I don't know. What?'

A MERMAID!

'I don't believe it!' exclaimed Mr Sign.
I BET YOU DON'T BELIEVE IT, BUT IT'S
TRUE AND I ENCLOSE THE EVIDENCE.
INSIDE THE BROWN ENVELOPE YOU
WILL FIND A PHOTOGRAPH TAKEN BY
ME THIS MORNING. IT'S OF THE SAME
MERMAID. I HOPE THIS WILL BE A
GOOD STORY FOR YOUR NEWSPAPER.

'It'll be a *great* story for my newspaper – if
it's true,' thought Mr Sign, fumbling for the
brown envelope that his secretary had
paper-clipped to the letter. He ripped open
the envelope and pulled out Hamlet's
instant photograph.

'Yippee! It's true, it's true! A mermaid! A
mermaid in Hammersmith!'

Mr Sign leapt to his feet clutching the
precious photograph and ran to his office
door. He flung the door open and called out
to his secretary, 'Miss Hazeldeane, hold the
front page!'

An hour ago Mr Sign was a most
unhappy man. Now he was the happiest
man in London, perhaps even the happiest

man in the world. He had been a journalist for ten whole years and he'd never had a world exclusive before. Now he had one and what a world exclusive it was!

Mr Sign set about writing the headline right away. He began with:

WORLD EXCLUSIVE
MERMAID PHOTOGRAPHED IN LONDON BATH

But after he had changed it at least ten times, he ended up with:

WORLD EXCLUSIVE
BOY MEETS MERMAID
– IN HAMMERSMITH

He spent the rest of the day writing the story to go with Hamlet's amazing photograph. By the time he had written the story and rewritten it and checked the

headline and double-checked it, it was time to go home. Tomorrow the paper would be published and his front-page story would be the talk of the town.

That evening the story of Hamlet Brown and the mermaid of Irving Terrace was the talk of the Sign household. Mrs Sarah Sign was a journalist like her husband, but she didn't work on a newspaper. She worked for a breakfast television company called TV-am.

'It's a wonderful story, Sam,' said Mrs Sign. 'But do you think it's true?'

'Of course it's true,' said Mr Sign.

'I know that hundreds of years ago sailors and people *said* they'd seen mermaids, but I don't think I've heard of one in the twentieth century,' said Mrs Sign. 'You don't think the boy's just imagining things?'

'If he's imagining things, then I'm imagining things too. I tell you, Sarah, I saw the photograph and there's no doubt in my mind that the creature in that bath was a real live mermaid. I'm a trained journalist,' Mr Sign went on, pulling himself up to his full height, 'and you can't pull the wool over my eyes.'

'I'm a trained journalist too,' smiled Mrs Sign, 'and I think there's something fishy going on.'

'Something fishy, Sarah?' chuckled Mr

Sign. 'Of course, a mermaid's fishy!' (He was very pleased with his little joke.)

'Well, if you're right, Sam, it's certainly a wonderful story and a great scoop for you and the paper. Well done.'

'Thank you,' said Mr Sign, giving his wife a bow.

'And if you have it as an exclusive in the paper tomorrow, perhaps we could have Hamlet Brown and his amazing mermaid on the programme on Friday. It would certainly be different.'

'It would be sensational!' said Mr Sign.

'I think I'll give Master Brown a telephone call,' said Mrs Sign.

'Good idea,' said her husband. 'I've got the number. But don't call now. It's getting late. Call him in the morning.'

'I will,' said Mrs Sign. And she did.

7. Hamlet Brown, TV star?

On Thursday morning, just as Mr and Mrs Brown and Hamlet and Susan were finishing their breakfast, the telephone rang at No. 13 Irving Terrace.

Mr Brown answered it and, as usual when Mr Brown answered the telephone, he pretended to be the butler in a very grand household. 'This is the Brown residence. Can I be of service?'

'Hello,' said Mrs Sign at the other end. 'Can I speak to Hamlet Brown please?'

'And whom shall I say is calling?' said Mr Brown.

'I'm Sarah Sign from TV-am.'

'Are you sure?' said Mr Brown, so surprised he nearly forgot his butler's voice.

'No, I'm not Shaw, I'm Sign, Sarah Sign
from TV-am, the breakfast television

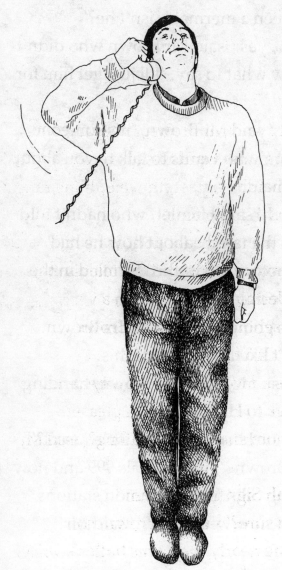

station, and I'd like to have a word with Hamlet Brown please. He *is* the young man who has seen a mermaid, isn't he?'

'Well, er, yes,' said Mr Brown who didn't quite know what to say. 'I'll just get him for you.'

'Hamlet,' said Mr Brown, 'it's someone from TV-am who wants to talk to you about your mermaid.'

'Oh good,' said Hamlet, who hadn't told anyone in the family about how he had taken a photograph of the mermaid in the bath. 'I'm coming.'

'What is going on?' asked Mrs Brown, who didn't like the sound of this.

'Don't ask me,' said Mr Brown, handing the receiver to Hamlet.

'What's he been up to, the little rascal?' said Mrs Brown. 'First he dials 999 and now he's getting calls from television stations.'

'I don't know what to say,' said Mr Brown.

Susan didn't have anything to say either.

When he came off the telephone, Hamlet had plenty to say. 'Great news!'

'What's that?' asked Mr Brown.

'I'm going to be on the telly,' said Hamlet.

'When?' said Mrs Brown, who could feel one of her headaches coming on.

'Tomorrow morning,' said Hamlet.

'But why?' spluttered Mrs Brown.

'Because of the mermaid, of course!' said Hamlet proudly.

'Oh, but Hamlet, dear son of mine,' said his father, 'there isn't any mermaid. 'Twas a figment of your imagination.'

'Oh yes there is a mermaid,' said Hamlet fiercely, 'and I can prove it.'

'How?' asked Mrs Brown.

'I took a photograph of her, sitting in the bath, combing her long golden hair with your best comb, Mum.'

'I wondered where it had got to,' said Mrs Brown.

'Well, where's the photograph then?' asked Mr Brown.

'I haven't got it,' said Hamlet.

'There!' said Susan all of a sudden. 'That shows he's lying.'

'No I'm not,' said Hamlet, turning on his sister. 'I haven't got the photograph

because I sent it to the newspaper. That's
how the TV people got to hear about it. It's
a real world exclusive.'

'Oh my,' said Mrs Brown, whose head
was really thumping now, 'whatever next?'

'Tidying up the breakfast things, that's
what's next,' said Mr Brown. 'Afterwards,
we'll all go for a jolly walk and clear the
cobwebs out of our heads.'

'We can't go out,' cried Hamlet. 'Mrs
Sign's coming round in a minute.'

'Who's Mrs Sign?' asked Mrs Brown
anxiously.

'The television lady,' said Hamlet.

'I thought she was Mrs Shaw,' said Mr
Brown who was getting very confused.

'She only lives round the corner,'
explained Hamlet. 'She wants to talk about
the programme. I'm going to be paid, you
know.'

'Paid, eh?' said Mr Brown who always
liked the sound of money.

'How much?' asked Susan who had been very quiet for a while.

'Forty pounds – so there!' said Hamlet, sticking his tongue out at his older sister.

'Now don't you two start again,' said Mrs Brown; 'I don't think my nerves will stand it.'

Just then the doorbell rang and poor Mrs Brown almost jumped out of her skin.

'What was that?' she squealed.

'Only the doorbell, dearest one,' said Mr Brown. 'I'll go.'

Mr Brown went to the front door and there was Mrs Sign.

'Oh yes,' said Mr Brown, 'you must be Mrs Shaw Sign.'

'Mrs Sarah Sign actually,' she said.

'Of course, of course,' said Mr Brown, who didn't really know what he was saying. 'Do come this way.'

Sarah Sign followed Mr Brown into the kitchen where Mr Brown offered her a chair

and Mrs Brown poured her a cup of tea.

'Now,' she said, getting out her pencil and notebook, 'tell me all about it.'

'It was like this –' began Hamlet.

'I'd like to explain –' said Mr Brown.

'You'll really have to forgive –' said Mrs Brown.

'Can I say something please?' said Susan.

They all spoke at once, so, of course, poor Sarah Sign couldn't understand a word.

'One at a time, please,' she said holding up her hand.

'Yes, yes, one at a time,' said Mrs Brown. 'In fact, I think Hamlet and I are the only ones who need to talk to Mrs Sign.'

'But Mum,' said Susan.

'But nothing, Susan,' said Mum. 'Off you go to your room and get on with your project.'

'But Mum, I've got something to say.'

'Not now, dear. Off you run, please.'

So Susan was sent up to her room and Mr Brown was turned from being the butler into being the gardener and sent out to the garden to look after his marrow.

'Now,' said Mrs Brown, when there was just her and Hamlet and the lady from TV-am sitting at the kitchen table, 'let's begin at the beginning. What has Hamlet done?'

'I'll tell you what I've done, Mum,' said Hamlet excitedly. 'I've taken a photograph of the mermaid. I managed to sneak up on her in the bathroom and surprise her.'

'But, Hamlet,' said Mrs Brown gently, 'mermaids only exist in story books and in films and in plays. Years ago I even acted the part of a mermaid in a play myself. It was great fun, but it was only play-acting. I'm sorry, Hamlet dear, but mermaids aren't real.'

'This one is,' said Hamlet as sure of himself as ever, 'and I've got a photograph to prove it.' He turned to Mrs Sign. 'I have got a photograph, haven't I?'

'Yes indeed,' said Sarah Sign. 'Here it is.' And from her briefcase she produced the latest edition of the *Hammersmith Times* and laid it out on the table for Hamlet and his mother to see. Mrs Brown read the headline

WORLD EXCLUSIVE
BOY MEETS MERMAID
– IN HAMMERSMITH

and her eyes went saucer-wide. She picked up the paper and took a close look at the photograph of the mermaid and her eyes nearly popped out of her head.

'Oh, Hamlet,' she gasped. 'That's not a mermaid – that's Susan!'

'What?' cried Hamlet.

'Who?' said Mrs Sign.

'Susan, Susan Brown, my daughter, Hamlet's sister. You can only just see her face behind that long blonde wig, but it's her all right.'

Mrs Brown put the paper down on the kitchen table, got up and went out into the hall. She called up the stairs, 'Susan, Susan Brown, come down here at once – at once do you hear me!'

Looking very sheepish, with head held low, poor Susan Brown came into the kitchen to face her mother and brother and Mrs Sign.

'What is the meaning of this, my girl?' said Mrs Brown looking crosser than Hamlet or Susan had ever seen her look.

'I tried to tell you, Mum, but you –'

'Don't answer back, Susan,' snapped her mother.

'It was only meant as a joke,' sniffed the unhappy girl.

'I don't think it's very funny,' said Hamlet.

'Where did you find the costume?' asked Mrs Brown sternly.

'In the attic.'

'And who said you could go up into the attic?'

'Nobody did.'

'Well, young lady, I'm telling you that you can go up there now and stay up there until you have tidied it all up. You can come down when you've cleaned every corner, wiped every surface, dusted every box, and not before. Do you hear me?'

'Yes, Mum.'

'And say "sorry" to your brother.'

'Sorry, Hamlet.' And having said 'sorry' to her brother and looking fairly sorry for herself as well, Susan made her way to the broom cupboard under the stairs to collect all the cleaning things she needed for her work in the attic.

'So it wasn't a real mermaid, after all,' said Mrs Sign, with a little sigh, putting her

pencil and her notepad back into her
briefcase.

'No, I'm afraid it was just my naughty
daughter dressing up in an old costume I'd
forgotten we'd even got in the attic.'

Mrs Sign got up to go. She put out her
hand for Hamlet to shake.

'I suppose you won't be wanting me on

the programme tomorrow, after all,' said Hamlet, looking very sad.

'I'm afraid not, Hamlet,' said Mrs Sign. 'No mermaid, no story.'

'No forty pounds,' said Hamlet.

'I'm sorry,' said Mrs Sign, and she was sorry too because she liked Hamlet and she liked having unusual items on her programme. 'Perhaps another time. Who knows?'

'Yes, indeed, who knows?' said Mrs Brown trying to be as jolly as possible as she showed Mrs Sign towards the hall. 'Ah, here's my husband to say goodbye.'

And here was Mr Brown, just in from the garden, but not at all able to shake hands with Mrs Sign because in his arms he was carrying his prize marrow – and it was ENORMOUS.

'Oh really,' said Mrs Brown who wasn't pleased to see Mr Brown tramping his muddy boots through the house.

'Isn't it a beauty?' said Mr Brown, happily ignoring his wife.

'It's magnificent,' said Mrs Sign who was

wide-eyed with amazement at the size of the prize marrow.

'I think it must be one of the biggest ever grown in Britain you know,' said Mr Brown rather proudly.

'Do you really, Dad?' said Hamlet.

'I do indeed, my boy,' said Mr Brown.

'Come along now, you two,' said Mrs Brown to her husband and son. 'Mrs Sign wants to get on her way. We've wasted enough of her time already. We mustn't hold her up any longer.'

'Oh not at all,' said Mrs Sign who was looking at the monster marrow admiringly. 'In fact, Mrs Brown, I don't think I do want to go just yet. Believe it or not, I've had rather an interesting idea...'

8. 'An Amazing Family!'

The next morning, at 8.30 a.m., when they had finished clearing away the breakfast dishes, Mrs Brown and Susan sat down in the sitting room at No. 13 Irving Terrace and turned on the television.

The news had just finished and there, on the TV-am sofa, were Jane Sparkle, wearing a very elegant televison presenter's dress, and Miles Dance, wearing a very jolly jumper and an even jollier grin to go with it. And, yes, sitting opposite them were Mr Brown and Hamlet Brown holding the biggest marrow you've ever seen.

'Good morning Britain,' said Jane. 'It's Friday morning and we've got something a little bit different to show you now.'

'Yes,' said Miles, 'today we thought we were going to be showing you an amazing mermaid photographed by this young man, Hamlet Brown, but the mermaid turned out to be his sister dressed up –'

'So instead,' continued Jane, 'Hamlet has brought along his father, a professional actor and amateur gardener, who has grown the largest marrow ever seen in

Britain! Hamlet, Mr Brown, tell us all about it.'

And Hamlet and Mr Brown told their story to Jane and to Miles and to people all over the country, including, of course, Mrs Brown and Susan.

In the sitting-room at No. 13 Irving Terrace, Mrs Brown turned to Susan with a smile and said, 'It was a naughty trick to play on Hamlet, but it has helped him earn forty pounds.'

'Will Dad get paid as well?' asked Susan.

'I expect so. He'll probably get into *The Guinness Book of Records*, too.'

'Hooray!' said Susan.

On the television Jane was saying, 'It's time now for a break. Our thanks to Hamlet and his father. The Browns are clearly an amazing family.'

Hamlet and his Dad smiled at the camera and held up the giant marrow with pride. Then on came the advertisements and

suddenly Hamlet and Mr Brown at the
television studio, and Mrs Brown and
Susan at No. 13, realized they were
listening to a voice they all knew rather well
... 'Try the tingle tongue taste test and
you'll find that tip-top Trolloppe's best
baked beans always beat the rest ...'

'Yes,' thought Mrs Brown, as she switched off the television, 'the Browns clearly are an amazing family!'

HELP!

Margaret Gordon

Fred and Flo are very helpful little pigs. The problem is, the more helpful they try to be, the more trouble they cause. Whether they are washing Grandad's car, looking after Baby or doing the decorating, disaster is never far away! Four hilarious stories featuring two very charming – and helpful – piglets.

DUMBELLINA

Brough Girling

What could be worse than the thought of moving house, changing school and leaving all your friends behind? When her Mum announces they are moving, Rebecca feels totally miserable – until she meets Dumbellina, the iron fairy.

ENOUGH IS ENOUGH

Margaret Nash

Usually when Miss Boswell uses her magic phrase, it works: Class 1 know that she means enough is *enough*, and get back to work, for a while at least. But when Miss Boswell's special plant begins to grow and grow until it has wiped the sums off the board, curled right out of the classroom and is heading for the kitchen, not even shouting 'Enough is enough!' will stop it!

BELLA'S DRAGON

Chris Powling

Two fantastic stories about ordinary children. In the first, Bella is surprised to see a dragon flop down into her back garden. School is closed and she's bored — what could be more fun than to help a lonely dragon find a new den? In the second story, Frankie makes a huge mistake when he meets a witch stuck in a ditch and gives her back her magic wand.

THE RAILWAY CAT AND THE HORSE

Phyllis Arkle

Alfie and his friends are very curious to learn that a valuable horse is going to be delivered to their station. Could it be a racehorse, they wonder? They soon find out that it's no ordinary horse, but one that's going to need very special treatment!

THE HODGEHEG

Dick King-Smith

The story of Max the hedgehog who become a hodgeheg, who becomes a hero. The hedgehog family of Number 5A are a happy bunch but they dream of reaching the Park across the road. Unfortunately, a very busy road lies between them and their goal and no one has found a way to cross it in safety. No one, that is, until the determined young Max decides to solve the problem once and for all . . .